Brian Wildsmith

DAISY

PANTHEON BOOKS   NEW YORK

Farmer Brown was a very hard
worker. Every day he worked in
his fields until the sun went
down. After his dinner he liked
to watch television. One night he
saw an advertisement for a shiny
new tractor. "I'd love to have a
machine like that," he thought.
"It would make my life much
easier."

Daisy his cow liked watching television too. She loved looking at all the exciting places outside the farm. "I wish I could see the whole world," she thought.

One day on his way home,
Farmer Brown forgot to close the
gate to Daisy's field.

He was so tired he didn't even watch television. He ate a small supper and then went straight to bed.

Daisy saw the open gate. She thought of all the wonderful places she had seen on television.

"Now is my chance," she thought
as she dashed out of the field.

Daisy wandered through the
countryside and at last she came
to a village. Part of the village
was built right into the side of a
hill.

"So this is the world," Daisy
thought as she walked off the
hillside and onto the rooftops.

But when she came to the edge of a roof, she was frightened and didn't know what to do. "Look at the cow on the roof," shouted the villagers. "How can we get her down?"

"That looks like Daisy," said the village priest. "Call Farmer Brown. He'll know what to do."

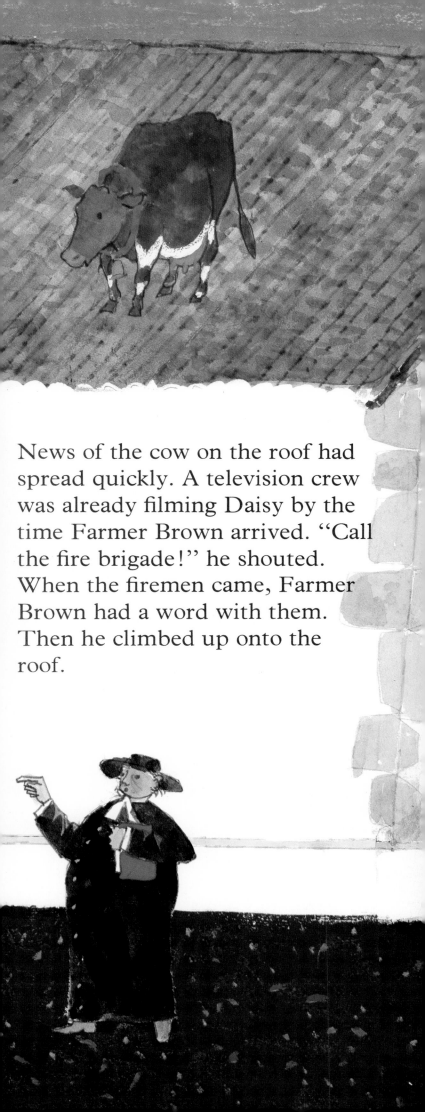

News of the cow on the roof had
spread quickly. A television crew
was already filming Daisy by the
time Farmer Brown arrived. "Call
the fire brigade!" he shouted.
When the firemen came, Farmer
Brown had a word with them.
Then he climbed up onto the
roof.

"Now Daisy," he said, "we are on television. So be a good girl and do as I tell you." Daisy looked at the cameras. "Now come on," he said. "Jump!" He gave her a big push and down she fell, safely into the firemen's net. "Back to the farm, Daisy. Your adventure is over," Farmer Brown said. Daisy was very sad.

A few days later, a film producer
called on Farmer Brown. "I saw
your cow on television," he said.
"She was great. I'd like to buy
her and make her a movie star."
"Daisy is not for sale!" said
Farmer Brown. "Then let me rent
her," said the producer. "All
right, but you must be kind to
her," said Farmer Brown. "It's a
deal," said the producer.

The next day Farmer Brown bought a shiny new tractor. The producer took Daisy to a nearby port. There she was hoisted aboard a ship and taken to Hollywood. "Now I will really see the world," thought Daisy.

In Hollywood everyone loved
Daisy.

She acted in many movies and soon became a big star.

Daisy's fame spread
very quickly. She was
on the cover of all the
best magazines.

She even appeared in a bubble-bath advertisement.

And great banquets were held in her honor. She was served all kinds of delicious food . . .

. . . caviar, smoked salmon, champagne, lemonade, ice cream and cake.

But Daisy grew tired of all this rich food. "Why don't they bring me some nice fresh grass and buttercups?" she thought.

"This is not proper food for a
cow to eat." And she kicked all
her food onto the floor.

Daisy began to grow thin. She became pale and sad, and the producer was very worried about her health. He took her to see a famous veterinarian.

"There's nothing much wrong with this cow," said the vet. "She's just homesick. A nice patch of grass and a rest in her old field would soon cure her."

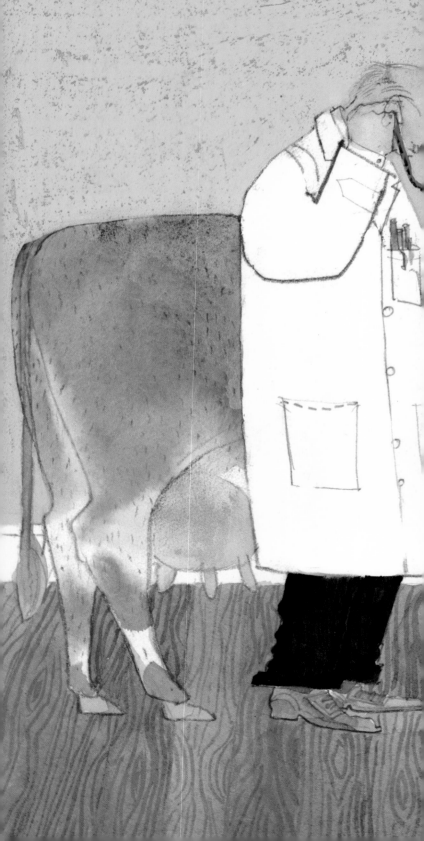

The producer was a kind man, and he had grown very fond of Daisy. It upset him to see her so sad. "All right, Daisy," he said, "we'll make one last movie. And it will be the most spectacular one of all."

The movie was called *Daisy Come Home*. In the last scene Daisy was flown on an airplane high in the sky.

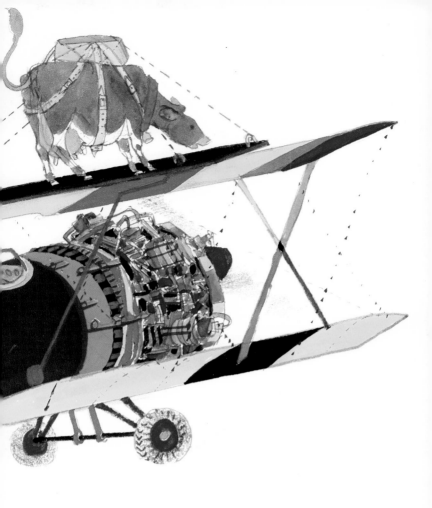

"Look Daisy," said the producer.
"There's your old field down
there. Now do as I say."

Daisy mooed with joy as she floated gently down through the air, going home.
She was overjoyed to be in her own field and to smell the grass and buttercups again. Just then Farmer Brown drove up in his shiny new tractor.
"It's wonderful to have you back," he said, throwing his arms around Daisy. "This field didn't seem the same without you. I've missed you!"

Together they went home. In the evenings they both watched television. Farmer Brown wasn't so tired now that he had his tractor.

And Daisy? She often thought of her adventurous days as a movie star. But now she was content to live where she really belonged.

*For my Mother
and my Father*

Copyright © 1984 by Brian Wildsmith
All rights reserved under International and Pan-American Copyright
Conventions. Published in the United States by Pantheon Books, a
division of Random House, Inc., New York. Published in
Great Britain by Oxford University Press.
Manufactured in Hong Kong

First American Edition

Library of Congress Cataloging in Publication Data
Wildsmith, Brian. Daisy.
Summary: A cow's dream of seeing the world comes true,
but it doesn't bring her happiness.
[1. Cows—Fiction]   I. Title.
PZ7.W647.Dai   1984   [E]   83-12150
ISBN 0-394-85975-8
ISBN 0-394-95975-2 (lib. bdg.)